Zion
World Order

By
Herman Hearl

Dedication

This book is dedicated for people and communities with alternative perspective and views to discover the world of Zion and its priory.

The material in this book can be damaging in terms of reputation to the elite class, but it's a pure fiction and should not be considered as something serious. The book encourages you to change your perspective and look into the depth of occult societies, especially if you became the victim of their projects and wish to fight back or know what to do.

About the Author

The author, born on May 3, 1993, has dedicated his life to battling secret societies by exposing their true nature and occult origins. He sheds light on occult societies and their inhumane actions toward ordinary people, often with the assistance of lesser-known political parties in Great Britain. In a quote attributed to the author, he states, "Secret societies have infiltrated our politics, our lives, and our business establishments, ultimately bringing war to our doorstep. We must expose them and reveal their true nature to the public, as they pose a significant threat to us. John F. Kennedy understood this danger; he risked his own life and paid the ultimate price. They do not discriminate based on status; if you pose a threat to them or their cause, they will take action and eliminate you."

I am a member of Zion, and I want to tell you about what is happening in the world order.

My story began in 1988; at that time, I was an investor in one of the big companies which specialised in gold mining, and my success resulted from occult deals between myself and other members of the society. In 1988, I joined a commercial organisation called Zion. It specialised in the provision of a platform to conclude large deals. Many successful businessmen were in it, also a part of the US Government personnel. My partner, who was working in the organisation, had offered me membership in the organisation in exchange for silence on how the deals were done, which was, as a matter of fact, the murder of innocent people.

People disappear, and there is an explanation for this, deliberately or by a matter of fate. However, in this particular instance, everything works like a mechanism.

Masons also practise kidnapping for such deals or equivalent by nature. I have sold my soul to the devil by joining Zion. The belief in occult practises, and ideology is an example of a "Sold-out nature" and inhumanity. Murder is their main priority, kidnapping people and executing occult operations on their victims. To achieve and establish a world order and the price for which death of innocent people. I was personally involved in the murder of an innocent person under the ritual sacrifice.

The system operates based on kidnapping the victim, filming occult content, as a result, a devil mathematical calculation of algorithms. During the victim's struggles for the so-called information, for a naive belief, for insurance between the participants of the ritual.

The rituals between the representatives of a business society and politicians varies by nature, depending on the type of deal. Everything is structured by a class type, from sexual orgies to a practical murder and a ritual sacrifice.

Zion does not personally specialise in kidnapping; this is what, by the rule, is commonly practised by the Masonic societies as well as the Illuminati. The choice of victim depends on a deal and ritual in which the victim will die a slow, painful death, be burned alive, or their hearts will be extracted in accordance with an ancient rule of Mayans.

Special divisions working in the governments of the United States of America, Germany, France and the United Kingdom specialise in projects involving kidnapping for occult rituals. The divisions cooperate with the participants of the deals as well as the media conglomerate, which projects the news to an audience; However, the fact is, they participate in a murder. The CIA and the British Intelligence Services all carry an occult nature and participate in deals to have insurance and securities for money and the principles of capitalism. By its nature, the current model of capitalism is a tool for outsourcing resources by concluding such deals.

For example, in the 911 attacks, members of a lower cast in comparison to Zion, Skull and Bones, in a deal with the US Government, thoughtfully committed mass murder, only to invade Iraq.

An occult format of the murders, victims aged 25 to 60, spy operations, vehicles with government number plates or angel numbers, acknowledged low cast members of occult societies, wearing various clothing and colours, uniforms, and media playing occult music, which is the modern genre. Provocative signals from brands and symbols.

It is called MK Ultra, which is a signal that you have been chosen for a sacrifice in the name of deals; as much as the winning formula in which the government wins, the media conglomerate is a beneficiary, for example, in the case of Skripals in the United Kingdom that were murdered after the so-called Novichok poisoning, in a ritual format.

The world order is based on sacrifices, and it is an essential part of it; it is practised in every country in an agreement with Zion.

In 1990, it is May, the Zion society is gathering in Mexico; the methodology is based on a Mayan sacrifice. The victim is a three-month-old baby who was kidnapped from a foster home. For the ceremony, an elite of the US business establishment, in which the Ford Family members were participating, the ritual clothing was in the style of an ancient Aztecs, including the instruments of heart extraction. There were cameras surrounding the pedestal.

It was a big deal between the representatives of BMW, Ford, Adidas and Bertelsmann. The nature of that deal was to settle any confrontations between the parties involved. They were the Western and Eastern Illuminati and representatives of the German National Party.

Their faces were not covered, to be recorded on camera and further for the content to be shared by one another.

I've seen the video and a report about this event personally.

The person who was chosen to commit the murder was Liz Mohn, a representative of the Bertelsmann Group. Firstly, ritual music began to play off the ancient Aztecs, and then a toddler was stripped naked and carried to the pedestal, all of which had happened at noon. Liz pulled the toddler's heart out; his blood was spilt in glasses and consumed by the participants.

In the world order, there is a concept of the clock by which the Zion members communicate. Societies have their own unique numbers; for example, take the German National Party; their clock represents the number seven, many of which came out from Nazi Germany, and even today, they follow a Nazi ideology, building their own world order or what they call a fourth Reich. Bertelsmann is not an exception; on their count, there are dozens of murdered victims, and their establishment individually specialises in programmes like MK Ultra, kidnapping and murdering innocent people in the name of personal gain and security. The Germans mostly burn their victims alive or boil them to death; this practice is from an infamous Ahnenerbe, and the concept came from Nazi Germany, which in fact, created the first killing structure in the name of a devil. By the clock, for example, the Rockefellers which is number nine and are considered to be the highest cast of Pendars.The pendar stands for the one that holds the pen or, in ancient days, the one that holds the feather, who has the capability to write history. The Rockefellers are quite isolated from the idea of ritual sacrifices, as they are wealthy and powerful enough not to take part in any security deals. While others deliberately choose to murder innocent people. The Illuminati are number nine and three by the clock, symbolising a pyramid, partially integrated with the Masons, the deal that was done in 1893, a shared world order in the United States of America, shared power over two primary secret societies. The masonic numbers vary in accordance with their colonial agenda and it goes anto-clockwise from twelve to ten. For example, the English heritage is twelve, such as establishments like the Bank of England, which today is still controlled by the masons; it started with France, ending the colonial cycles with England, Scotland, Canada and the United States.

Masons did not practise ritual murders until 1955, although they did kill their own members in the past; by that time, the reforms were made, and their hybrid Masonic-Illuminati society was formed, which turned into an occult sacrificial concept involving kidnapping and murders.

In 1932, Fords, Baruchs and representatives from the Anglo-Scottish coalition adopted a memorandum, which was a concept of equilibrium. Every cycle, the big businesses agreed to steal the taxpayer's money from the civilians. Equilibrium is a model by which the deals affect geopolitics and international affairs. Every cycle meant a choice of an opponent for military purposes, such as the Nazi Germany. By investing in Germany, to be more precise, in the Bavarian Elite, the coalition could manipulate processes in the National Party's establishment and the rise of fascism in

Germany. Slowly but surely, growing my own potential on the market and own businesses, as well as accumulating profit from foreign investments. Such a format of equilibrium works even today; the war in Ukraine is an agreement between the Western elites, the United States, the United Kingdom, Germany and France.

The government and businesses had an agreement with the Zion branch to extract the taxpayer's funds for the war effort in Ukraine. The money will be split between the elites when they will be withdrawn by the Ukrainian politicians. Participants such as the UK, US, Germany and France had established the new political elites in Ukraine after the events of the euro-maidan. The price, death of the Ukrainians, and equilibrium which is built on bloodshed and sacrifice. As an instrument, the right-wing neo-Nazi groups were chosen, which followed Nazi ideology. Germany is a direct investor in such groups. The Zion also has a structure adopted for the Zionist elites. According to the deal, Zion must invest in another equilibrium by provoking Palestine and having further manslaughter since Palestine was chosen as an instrument of mass murder and a theft of taxpayers' money on the war effort.

The Zionists do take part in MK Ultra and human sacrifices.

Zionists control the Federal Reserve of the United States of America, in an agreement with the democratical party, Joe Biden, to execute equilibrium has been involved in deals with the Ukrainian government in mediation with the Germans. We should not forget that Germany and their ambition for unification in order to build the fourth Reich became the fathers of sacrificial concepts.

Monopoly and murders, blood that flows through the establishment; for example, take BMW, which has murdered one particular engineer and stolen his invention. His name was Stanley Allen Meyer; the contract was executed through a specialist division of a hired squad from Albania at the end of the nineties. BMW acquired the technology and saved it for themselves. Another murder, and the victim has died from cyanide poisoning. The system is slowly losing its grip on things; what was possible before became less of a possibility today and turned into a risk. Acknowledged members who take part in sacrifices through Zion, most of whom are famous entrepreneurs, artists, and musicians who sold themselves in the name of murder, are also captured on the camera. Consume and erode the population through sexualisation, the inception of none traditional values, fetishism, and masochism, to aim for capital gain by causing conflicts, wars and murders.

Murders with a lack of human touch, such cruelty and yet manage to steal their victim's identities, changing their entire history cover-ups, implying a variety of the murder versions. For example, Sarah Everard was sacrificed by the British Government.

By setting up their own employee who was a mason and a policeman. Masons do sacrifice their brothers in the name of deals through Zion, as well as take part in the equilibrium and deaths of innocent people, despite their reputation and an attempt to show themselves from a good side by donating money to charities. Zion has a system of the slave trade, which involves kidnapping for exploitation and organ black market. Often you would see the health care organisations working closely with the commercial structures and the government entities. The victims are carefully chosen in accordance with their health records, blood type, and the quality and function of their organs. As a result, the victims end up dead through strangling or drowning; the methodology is created and functioning in this industry. The organs are being sold on the black market or by the individual preference, delivered to a person of interest. The ones that were saved from such fate end up in secret prisons in the Sahara desert, Egypt, Central Africa and Australia, where they live as prisoners in a prison colony.

The principle is based on the benefits of saving a particular individual: if you are lucky to live, you end up in Heaven; if you are chosen for the ritual, you die in Hell. According to statistics, Germany is leading in top major MK Ultra equivalent programmes through Zion, ritual sacrifices and the reason for it, their attempt to create unity to build up their fourth economic reich; more of the victims, the better.

Let's head up to the eastern concept of monopoly and their own concept of Zion, in which the governing parties get rid of the individuals that are not suitable for their agenda views or can be an opposing force. In the Russian Federation, there is a system by which the sacrifices are executed. The followers of Ahnenerbe escaped to the Soviet Union at the end of the war, undercover as civilians and allocated their lives to farming, their concepts of sacrifices were adopted by the Soviet Agro Union and then by the Russian Elites.

The monopoly on technologies started right after the fall of the Soviet Union, and tendencies of Zion were adopted in the newly established government. There was an agreement made to murder the scientists under mysterious circumstances. The elite had decided to implement their own corrupt infrastructure in the Russian government. In which the elections were falsified, and there is only one major winning party. Contract murders were executed by a separate division working for the FSB. The political opponents that represent themselves or the Western coalition members end up dead or nowhere to be found. Again, through an agreement, in this case, Alexey Navalny who was suspected to be a member of the infamous Skull and Bones society, which is controlled through Yale University in the United States.

His death was a poisoning, and a political threat was liquidated, not to mention a fabricated case against him.

The death of Evgeniy Prigozhin, a bomb attached to a plane by the Belarussian special division. Powe and paranoia dictate the policies of FSB-covered Elites. However, from a political perspective, they are correct in terms of the war in Ukraine since it is a platform for the execution of equilibrium. The Russian Federation has never practised equilibrium as the United States and their allies do. The Chinese Republic has its own equivalent to Zion, in which the main priorities are based on kidnapping for organ transplantation and only direct murders are executed. The demonic powers and occultism are just a curtain for security, an ideology and belief, what is practised by those who believe in demons whilst the elites murder for a common capital gain. How deep are the cults in the government infrastructure? Zion is only a higher cast; everything else depends on those who write history, the Pendars. Human greed, selling soul for benefit, ordinary people do not notice those things which are hidden. You do not need to be a psychologist or have a qualification; you need to have a heart and soul.

My soul was taken over by greed and an ambition to have more money, although I think it is my duty to tell you about what is happening to you, an ordinary individual. As was mentioned before, Germany stands at the top of the rankings by quantity of murders. I will tell you about one particular project that is directly curated by the Bertelsmann Group in accordance with an equivalent programme to MK Ultra, which Zion is using. Drama, theatre, music and arts are the main schemes for performing psy-operations upon the victims. The Germans, in cooperation with the Spanish companies, their first Enigma project; Michael Cretu, composer and author of music associated with the new age genre, has created a mechanism by which the information of rituals, murders and ceremonies are being transferred between the parties involved. The songs are written in accordance with various scenarios implied to the victims, in combination with carefully crafted life scenarios through acknowledged members of occult societies.

Every album represents a victim of the project, often by quantities and depending on an initial investment in such operations. You can make an assumption that it is not profitable; however, their victims are in good health and are suitable candidates for the organ black market. There is nothing spiritual in this music; the lyrics motivate and coordinate an individual into a trap from which there is no escape. The continuation of the project was executed and passed on to German producer Andre Tannenberger at the end of the nineties; this project is also known as a research by which the German elites conclude their dirty deals; the death toll exceeds two thousand from the Enigma project.

There are currently changes taking place in the world order and not everyone tends to agree with the concept of equilibrium as well as MK Ultra programmes. Openly against it are the French Rothschilds who, for the last sixty years, have been opposing it and threatening to expose everything, although they participated with equilibrium in World War Two. As everything is connected, it would become a risk of exposure for the crimes committed against ordinary people and humanity. The Rothschilds are hated by both the Western and Eastern Illuminati for their independence and discard to participate in occult deals. The concept of occultism has various beliefs, although every belief is used to gain profit. For example, the belief in UFOs and extraterrestrials sacrifices in the name of god for prosperity. Belief in supernatural concepts works as a mechanism of distracting the population from more important topics, spreading lies and financially benefiting from it. An example is an occult case of the disappearance of an individual in Brazil how to turn the victim into a member of an occult society and earns money, later only to hide the real history behind this charade. Bruno Borges is an example in which an equal to our own system works on a practical level, a murder and cover-up on the government level, in which the president was involved. Occult sacrifice of a young student who was never interested in mythology, history or psychology; after his abduction with a use similar to the MK Ultra program, a decision was made to fully cover up his existence and twist it in accordance with what was a suitable story at the time. The police, which was, in fact, a special division which worked for the government entities, falsified those facts and turned Bruno into a book character.

After the investigation, all which could be witnessed, from the books, encryption and mysterious statue in his home, was fake, specifically made for the media conglomerate and, as a consequence, only to present Bruno as being alive and well. He and his parents were murdered whilst everyone else was watching his CGI version, talking about his new book.

Zion is not the only organisation that specialises in MK Ultra programmes or equivalent. For example, there is another separate infrastructure which specialises in occult programmes such as "The Writers Network" and book publishers. Working internationally often has connections with the elites and beneficiaries. They write a story with its primary scenario for the victims; the lower cast follows an ideology and belief in Satanism, which is a perfect serving instrument for the elites.

The Zionists, as an example, the leader of the Labour Party in Great Britain, Sir Keir Starmer, serves an international zionist congress and is sponsored by indirect third parties involved. He personally takes part in various occult ceremonies involving sexual orgies. However, the orgies are common in the British Elite Societies as much as the Royal Family. In their basis is esoteric sciences, occultism, which is chosen for the victims. An example is the case of Max Spiers, a conspiracy theorist who was investigating a world order and had a belief in the supernatural. He was often criticising the British Rothschilds and even exposed them as being Pendars which is true. He was selected to be in the MK Ultra program in Poland. Although for his criticism, the decision was made to murder him through blood poisoning. He was poisoned by a powerful substance; the contract was executed through the Zion branch in Poland in an agreement with the Zionist International Congress. He was selected at an early stage whilst attending St Edmunds University, which resulted in his candidacy as a victim since this institution had a direct link to the ZIC. The death of conspiracy theorists part of the public shows their belief in the supernatural, an instrument which is attached to the fantasy. Every ruler has blood on their hands, especially those that run European countries and America.

Securities, deals, human stupidity, a lobby of pedophiles of Westminster and the church, everything which is hidden behind the scenes. The Royal Family, by its own stupidity, takes part in this dirty show.

At the end of the nineties, a group of American entrepreneurs had created their own concept of securities, which was based on the sexual exploitation of victims, children and kidnapping. Establishment, which had some of the most notorious people, such as Bill Clinton and Jeffrey Epstein. Epstein has created a network to kidnap children, mainly girls aged twelve.

Sexual orgies were taken place on a private island in which a delegation of the political elites was present. The Royal Family was offered to participate in the deal in exchange for securities as insurance, and video material was shared between the participants in the hands of Epstein. He was eventually murdered by the prison guards, who were paid by the establishment, as he was a key witness in the court case and could have exposed everyone involved in the satanic rituals.

Dirty structure of the world order, who are we? We are eleven members by the clock since an old world order and pendars, which were number three, had given up their power. In the following pages, you will find out more about those who are involved in murders, research and which parties they belong to.

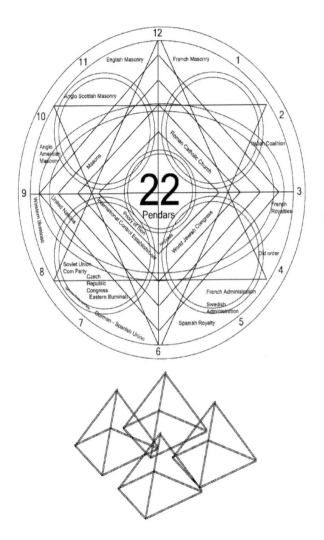

Silvia Renate Sommerlath

Eastern Iluiminati

Code:566648888365B394

Research Groups: No

Securities: Yes

Role: Pendar

Watch:5

Murders:12

Genre: Occult

Carl XVI Gustaf

Eastern Iluiminati

Code:088883758482939

Research Groups: No

Securities: Yes

Role: Pendar

Watch:5

Murders:25

Genre: Occult

Felipe VI

Eastern Iluiminati

Code:4738920934672888

Research Groups: No

Securities: Yes

Role: Pendar

Watch:6

Murders:13

Genre: Occult

Letizia Ortiz Rocasolano

Eastern Iluiminati

Code:66648739578390888

Research Groups: No

Securities: Yes

Role: Pendar

Watch:5

Murders:1

Genre: Occult

Charles III

Eastern Iluiminati

Code:462522294308887

Research Groups: Yes

Securities: Yes

Role: Spreading light

Watch:7

Murders:57

Genre: Occult

Duke of Kent

Mason

Code:476583937004728

Research Groups: Yes

Securities: Yes

Role: Grand Master

Watch:11

Murders:46

Genre: Occult

George W Bush

Skull and Bones

Code:999563758936738409

Research Groups: Yes

Securities: Yes

Role: Enforcer

Watch:9

Murders:3

Genre: Occult

Larry Fink

Western Illuminati

Code:0099473857392954090

Research Groups: No

Securities: No

Role: Spreading light

Watch:9

Murders:0

Genre: Enterprise

George Soros

Western Illuminati

Code:77770299990877802

Research Groups: No

Securities: No

Role: Spreading light

Watch:9

Murders:0

Genre: Enterprise

Bill Clinton

Western Illuminati

Code:4637589994837211483

Research Groups: Yes

Securities: Yes

Role: Spreading light

Watch:9

Murders:9

Genre: Occult

Hillary Clinton

Western Illuminati

Code:465674738212999039482

Research Groups: Yes

Securities: Yes

Role: Spreading light

Watch:9

Murders:7

Genre: Occult

William J. Burns

Western Illuminati

Code:01124958374893093

Research Groups: Yes

Securities: Yes

Role: Spreading light

Watch:9

Murders:3

Genre: Occult

Mervyn Davies

Skull and Bones

Code:9991070049284920O239

Research Groups: Yes

Securities: Yes

Role: Enforcer

Watch:10.7

Murders:2

Genre: Occult

Keir Starmer

International Jewish Congress

Code:550126648379O275849

Research Groups: No

Securities: No

Role: Enforcer

Watch:10

Murders:0

Genre: Enterprise

Richard Branson

Western Illuminati

Code:9999666601546382921

Research Groups: No

Securities: No

Role: Spreading light

Watch:9

Murders:0

Genre: Enterprise

Carsten Spohr

German National Party

Code:778880122146574382

Research Groups: Yes

Securities: Yes

Role: Pendar

Watch:7

Murders:15

Genre: Occult

Stefan Quandt

German National Party

Code:003856377463777583493

Research Groups: Yes

Securities: Yes

Role: Pendar

Watch:7

Murders:14

Genre: Occult

Hannelore Kraft

German National Party

Code:0647377739482930

Research Groups: Yes

Securities: Yes

Role: Enforcer

Watch:7

Murders:2

Genre: Occult

William Clay Ford Jr

Western Illuminati

Code:0047364999888037832

Research Groups: Yes

Securities: Yes

Role: Pendar

Watch:9

Murders:27

Genre: Occult

Tony Brair

Skull and Bones

Code:9990664738573423123364

Research Groups: No

Securities: No

Role: Enforcer

Watch:9

Murders:0

Genre: Enterprise

Gordon Brown

Western Illuminati

Code:0465376483947211675478839

Research Groups: No

Securities: No

Role: Spreading light

Watch:9

Murders:0

Genre: Enterprise

Bill Koch

Western Illuminati

Code:9994857362111854749930

Research Groups: Yes

Securities: Yes

Role: Spreading light

Watch:9

Murders:4

Genre: Occult

Rupert Murdoch

Independent

Code:6666684637829038271482

Research Groups: Yes

Securities: Yes

Role: Pendar

Watch:9

Murders:11

Genre: Occult

Murat Ulker

Mason

Code:1111100006453754848231

Research Groups: Yes

Securities: Yes

Role: Grandmaster

Watch:11

Murders:3

Genre: Occult

Herbert Hainer

German National Party

Code:7300000188887777

Research Groups: Yes

Securities: Yes

Role: Pendar

Watch:7.3

Murders:20

Genre: Occult

John Clifton Bogle

Western Illuminati

Code:8889990382983012

Research Groups: Yes

Securities: Yes

Role: Pendar

Watch:9

Murders:111

Genre: Occult

Jacob Rothschild

International Jewish Congress

Code:1483930004983

Research Groups: Yes

Securities: Yes

Role: Pendar

Watch:7

Murders:35

Genre: Occult

Jacqueline Mars

Western Illuminati

Code:47586666111385943038

Research Groups: Yes

Securities: Yes

Role: Spreading light

Watch:9

Murders:10

Genre: Occult

Ulf Mark Schneider

German National Party

Code:77777038218547573820l

Research Groups: Yes

Securities: Yes

Role: Enforcer

Watch:7

Murders:5

Genre: Occult

Dieter Schwarz

German National Party

Code:77777701294628392211O9

Research Groups: Yes

Securities: Yes

Role: Enforcer

Watch:7

Murders:15

Genre: Occult

Liz Mohn

German National Party / Origin: Ananerbe

Code:7300088812974839

Research Groups: Yes

Securities: Yes

Role: Pendar

Watch:7

Murders:8

Genre: Occult

William Anderson

German National Party

Code:7677745830933

Research Groups: Yes

Securities: No

Role: Enforcer

Watch:7

Murders:0

Genre: Occult

Ulrich Böckmann

German National Party

Code:77746352748209

Research Groups: Yes

Securities: Yes

Role: Enforcer

Watch:7

Murders:5

Genre: Occult

Lars Rebien Sørensen

Eastern Illuminati

Code:76777455501473823921

Research Groups: Yes

Securities: Yes

Role: Spreading light

Watch:7

Murders:9

Genre: Occult

William Worthington Bain Jr

Western Illuminati

Code:08466642371234123843728

Research Groups: Yes

Securities: Yes

Role: Spreading light

Watch:9

Murders:3

Genre: Occult

Albert Bourla

Western Illuminati

Code:06666473611113849994O374

Research Groups: Yes

Securities: Yes

Role: Spreading light

Watch:9

Murders:15

Genre:Enterprise

Joe Biden

Western Illuminati

Code:7716351003766699994555372

Research Groups: Yes

Securities: Yes

Role: Spreading light

Watch:9

Murders:5

Genre: Occult

Barack Obama

Western Illuminati

Code:9388899904738261728349

Research Groups: No

Securities: Yes

Role: Spreading light

Watch:9

Murders:2

Genre: Occult

David Cameron

Western Illuminati

Code:88806525141268727709215

Research Groups: Yes

Securities: Yes

Role: Spreading light

Watch:9

Murders:0

Genre: Enterprise

Frank Walter Steinmeier

German National Party

Code:191977771144141036525527

Research Groups: Yes

Securities: Yes

Role: Enforcer

Watch:7

Murders:1

Genre: Occult

Roland Busch

German National Party

Code:77735126110937463719

Research Groups: Yes

Securities: Yes

Role: Enforcer

Watch:7

Murders:5

Genre: Occult

Bernard Arnault

Eastern Illuminati

Code:777766011444550129481㦲

Research Groups: No

Securities: Yes

Role: Spreading light

Watch:7

Murders:14

Genre: Occult

Emmanuel Macron

Eastern Illuminati

Code:77704755516382910475B

Research Groups: No

Securities: No

Role: Spreading light

Watch:7

Murders:0

Genre: Enterprise

Ingvar Kamprad

Western Illuminati

Code:999047561112749II574B39

Research Groups: Yes

Securities: Yes

Role: Spreading light

Watch:9

Murders:25

Genre: Occult

Axel Aumuller

German National Party

Code:15777736471003B475III2303

Research Groups: Yes

Securities: Yes

Role: Enforcer

Watch:7

Murders:3

Genre: Occult

Samuel Walton

Western Illuminati

Code:0009996661284712623B9

Research Groups: Yes

Securities: Yes

Role: Spreading light

Watch:9

Murders:12

Genre: Occult

George Hearst

Western Illuminati

Code:11106544541211083728

Research Groups: Yes

Securities: Yes

Role: Spreading light

Watch:9

Murders:3

Genre: Occult

Karen Pritzker

Western Illuminati

Code:488819992746183010026l

Research Groups: Yes

Securities: Yes

Role: Spreading light

Watch:9

Murders:2

Genre: Occult

Klaus Kuhne

German National Party

Code:0777743561187453274

Research Groups: Yes

Securities: Yes

Role: Enforcer

Watch:7

Murders:10

Genre: Occult

Reinhold Wurth

Independent

Code:55637103817483912021

Research Groups: No

Securities: No

Role: Businessman

Watch:7

Murders:0

Genre: Enterprise

Georg Schaeffler

German National Party

Code:7778888064755514422231

Research Groups: Yes

Securities: Yes

Role: Spreading light

Watch: 7

Murders:4

Genre: Occult

Michael O Leary

Western Illuminati

Code:56553198735091743821

Research Groups: No

Securities: No

Role: Spreading light

Watch:9

Murders:0

Genre:Enterprise

Donald J Trump

Independent

Code:88880046661645371829137

Research Groups: No

Securities: No

Role: Enforcer

Watch:0

Murders:0

Genre:Enterprise

Alexandra Schorghuber

German National Party

Code:95457777111053621751

Research Groups: Yes

Securities: Yes

Role: Enforcer

Watch:7

Murders:1

Genre: Occult

Francoise Meyers

Eastern Illuminati

Code:05573144837102394728381 92

Research Groups: Yes

Securities: Yes

Role: Spreading light

Watch:7

Murders:4

Genre: Occult

Inigo Ucin

Western Illuminati

Code:6666600093657144289 1047

Research Groups: Yes

Securities: Yes

Role: Spreading light

Watch:6

Murders:2

Genre: Occult

Jacob Stausholm

Eastern Illuminati

Code:4421111047582536183123

Research Groups: No

Securities: No

Role: Spreading light

Watch:7

Murders:0

Genre:Enterprise

Amancio Ortega

Eastern Illuminati

Code:77776666619948814161423

Research Groups: Yes

Securities: Yes

Role: Spreading light

Watch:6

Murders:12

Genre: Occult

Nicolas Puech

Eastern Illuminati

Code:111230043536809477711

Research Groups: Yes

Securities: Yes

Role: Spreading light

Watch:7

Murders:16

Genre: Occult

Alexandre Vandamme

German National Party

Code:55555777702645123123064

Research Groups: Yes

Securities: Yes

Role: Enforcer

Watch:7

Murders:5

Genre: Occult

Charlene de Carvalho Heineken

German National Party

Code:05192555534132109183712З

Research Groups: Yes

Securities: Yes

Role: Enforcer

Watch:7

Murders:10

Genre: Occult

Vladimir Putin

Independent

Code:000000081788880111123

Research Groups: No

Securities: No

Role: Enforcer

Watch:6

Murders:0

Genre:Enterprise

Rishi Sunak

Western Illuminati

Code:98705157319473193028175В4

Research Groups: No

Securities: No

Role: Spreading light

Watch:9

Murders:0

Genre:Enterprise

Clemens Tonnies

German National Party

Code:71777770056212347708

Research Groups: Yes

Securities: Yes

Role: Enforcer

Watch:7

Murders:5

Genre: Occult

Rafael del Pino Calvo-Sotelo

Eastern Illuminati

Code:666666051517888810437121

Research Groups: No

Securities: Yes

Role: Spreading light

Watch:6

Murders:3

Genre: Occult

Melker Schorling

Eastern Illuminati

Code:55830193810111138888899101

Research Groups: Yes

Securities: Yes

Role: Spreading light

Watch:7

Murders:11

Genre: Occult

Antti Herlin

Western Illuminati

Code:888807743156104918

Research Groups: Yes

Securities: Yes

Role: Spreading light

Watch:9

Murders:10

Genre: Occult

Arvind Krishna

Western Illuminati

Code:109999055110932566

Research Groups: Yes

Securities: Yes

Role: Spreading light

Watch:9

Murders:2

Genre: Occult

Carlos Slim Helu

Independent

Code:009845557236666012349357

Research Groups: Yes

Securities: Yes

Role: Enforcer

Watch:6

Murders:15

Genre: Occult

Alain Wertheimer

Western Illuminati

Code:511900405748129481291

Research Groups: Yes

Securities: Yes

Role: Spreading light

Watch:9

Murders:13

Genre: Occult

Alison Kirkby

Mason

Code:1110555507421358036121

Research Groups: Yes

Securities: Yes

Role: Enforcer

Watch:11

Murders:2

Genre: Occult

Marc David Gunther Fielmann

Western Illuminati

Code:9999777019482371838919481

Research Groups: Yes

Securities: Yes

Role: Spreading light

Watch: 9

Murders:1

Genre: Occult

Mathias Dopfner

German National Party

Code:0077765878745356140991

Research Groups: Yes

Securities: Yes

Role: Enforcer

Watch:7

Murders:2

Genre: Occult

Roman Abramovich

Independent

Code:7119666609545321107817

Research Groups: No

Securities: No

Role: Enforcer

Watch:6

Murders:0

Genre: Enterprise

Suleiman Usmanov

Independent

Code:7666112131260548192782

Research Groups: No

Securities: No

Role: Enforcer

Watch:6

Murders:10

Genre: Enterprise

Jacob Aarup Andersen

German National Party

Code:78907777755555111312065

Research Groups: Yes

Securities: Yes

Role: Enforcer

Watch:7

Murders:13

Genre: Occult

Stefani Oessina

Eastern Illuminati

Code:05674201758034583914711891

Research Groups: No

Securities: No

Role: Spreading light

Watch:6

Murders:0

Genre: Enterprise

Kjeld Kirk Kristiansen

Western Illuminati

Code:8888099974612545454545411

Research Groups: Yes

Securities: Yes

Role: Spreading light

Watch:9

Murders:3

Genre: Occult

Phil Knight

Western Illuminati

Code:00009999666623524728811

Research Groups: No

Securities: No

Role: Spreading light

Watch:9

Murders:0

Genre: Enterprise

Warren Buffett

Western Illuminati

Code:4447699907713101111719

Research Groups: Yes

Securities: Yes

Role: Spreading light

Watch:9

Murders:8

Genre: Occult

Leonard Blavatnik

Western Illuminati

Code:666605437321180219451

Research Groups: No

Securities: Yes

Role: Spreading light

Watch:9

Murders:1

Genre: Occult

Gina Rinehart

Eastern Illuminati

Code:666660139158311104521

Research Groups: Yes

Securities: Yes

Role: Pendar

Watch:6

Murders:13

Genre: Occult

Peter Salovey

Skull and Bones

Code:9990167453019477583661029

Research Groups: Yes

Securities: Yes

Role: Enforcer

Watch:9

Murders:4

Genre: Occult

Sherry Brydson

Mason

Code:110351192115195301101

Research Groups: Yes

Securities: Yes

Role: Enforcer

Watch:11

Murders:4

Genre: Occult

Miriam Adelson

Independent

Code:445793481938176390122

Research Groups: Yes

Securities: Yes

Role: Enforcer

Watch:6

Murders:2

Genre: Occult

August Von Finck Jr

German National Party

Code:07777112564319530991

Research Groups: Yes

Securities: Yes

Role: Enforcer

Watch:7

Murders:3

Genre: Occult

Heinz Hermann Thiele

German National Party

Code:00077771119374B2718901

Research Groups: Yes

Securities: Yes

Role: Enforcer

Watch:7

Murders:4

Genre: Occult

Ariane de Rothschild

Eastern Illuminati

Code:007777777001

Research Groups: No

Securities: No

Role: Pendar

Watch:7

Murders:0

Genre:Enterprise

Bill Gates

Western Illuminati

Code:99927846723737738

Research Groups: Yes

Securities: Yes

Role: Spreading light

Watch:9

Murders:4

Genre: Occult

David Rockefeller Jr

Western Illuminati

Code:9999002066601

Research Groups: No

Securities: No

Role: Pendar

Watch:9

Murders:0

Genre: Enterprise

Mikhail Khodorkovsky

Western Illuminati

Code:866609991037838189231891

Research Groups: No

Securities: No

Role: Spreading light

Watch:9

Murders:0

Genre: Enterprise

Eyal Ofer

International Jewish Congress

Code:06655554833330164531289O

Research Groups: Yes

Securities: Yes

Role: Enforcer

Watch:6

Murders:5

Genre: Occult

Sharon White

Mason

Code:111175321109977181414143

Research Groups: Yes

Securities: No

Role: Enforcer

Watch:11

Murders:0

Genre: Occult

August Inselkammer Jr

German National Party

Code:77708135655501291481

Research Groups: Yes

Securities: Yes

Role: Pendar

Watch:7

Murders:1

Genre: Occult

Ernst August von Hannover

German National Party

Code:00000777788800132111

Research Groups: Yes

Securities: Yes

Role: Pendar

Watch:7

Murders:23

Genre: Occult

Ursula von der Leyen

German National Party

Code:564102977422102918301

Research Groups: No

Securities: No

Role: Enforcer

Watch:7

Murders:0

Genre: Occult

Stefan Hartung

German National Party

Code:07777766661230445876421

Research Groups: Yes

Securities: Yes

Role: Enforcer

Watch:7

Murders:4

Genre: Occult

Mark Zuckerberg

International Jewish Congress

Code:550166612091651594799912

Research Groups: Yes

Securities: Yes

Role: Enforcer

Watch:9

Murders:2

Genre: Occult

Bernd Lucke

German National Party

Code:01366521110191087777

Research Groups: Yes

Securities: Yes

Role: Enforcer

Watch:7

Murders:1

Genre: Occult

Richard Trice

Mason

Code:01155099916314413086

Research Groups: Yes

Securities: Yes

Role:Grandmaster

Watch:11

Murders:1

Genre: Occult

James Dimon

Western Illuminati

Code:1354225220066661101321

Research Groups: Yes

Securities: Yes

Role: Spreading light

Watch:9

Murders:5

Genre: Occult

Linda Thorell Hills

Mason

Code:01237819014465128811

Research Groups: Yes

Securities: Yes

Role:Retired

Watch:11

Murders:3

Genre: Occult

Duke of Marlborough

Western Illuminati

Code:5555001431276110043

Research Groups: Yes

Securities: Yes

Role: Pendar

Watch:9

Murders:7

Genre: Occult

Marie Warburg

International Jewish Congress

Code:66666015432194811156

Research Groups: Yes

Securities: Yes

Role: Pendar

Watch:6

Murders:1

Genre: Occult

Michael Knitter

German National Party

Code:934202313253940077712

Research Groups: Yes

Securities: Yes

Role: Enforcer

Watch:7

Murders:1

Genre: Occult

The occult research organisations served as a key element of the MK-Ultra program, which is common in Great Britain. Members of the organisation participate in collective deals with an element of kidnapping and delivery to private entities. The Baruchs and their organisations spread throughout the island, although there are many others, such as Masonic research lodges and

Anglo-German organisations. The structure is based on a secretarial segment of control; commonly, these are the so-called "Agro Families" which serve the occult society. Here is the shortlist.

Hartrott Nominees Limited

Times 1292 Limited

EAC Secretaries Limited

Form 10 Secretaries Limited

Writers in Prison Network Limited

Chalfen Secretaries Limited

L & A Secretaries Limited

Swift Incorporations

The Wizzard Group Limited

Temple Secretaries Limited

Domainscape Secretaries Limited

By the method of mathematical calculations, members communicate with one another as well as using Enigma encryption, transferring data in regards to their victims. The count of deaths exceeds a toll of three thousand people, including kidnapped children for the occult rituals. Everything happens in an agreement with the British Intelligence Services as they themselves are involved in occult murders. As an example, we will take an intelligence agent who was apparently murdered, although he was kidnapped by the British intelligence service and was sentenced to death through a ritual. It was an order from the Royal Family, and his name was Gareth Williams; he was working for MI5 and was selected by the Royals for murder. He was murdered in a ritual ceremony in which his heart was extracted; his blood was spilt. Into a jar and sent over to Her Majesty the Queen; although she did not participate directly in his murder, she carried that burden until her death. His organs were sold on the black market. These operations have a common pattern: victims are led to a critical point of paranoia, which results in victims searching for an exit by running away, whilst the members of cults work on their plan.

The victims usually order a taxi or a cab, whilst the driver is a member of a cult and drives the victim to a desired location, a remote place where they are greeted by other cult members and representatives of an organisation with their own transport, which is usually a black van. Then, the victim is sedated through a powerful sedative and insulin, after which their hands and legs are tightened up, and they are blindfolded. The victim is more or less in a weak state, paralysed. Furthermore, they take their victims to a forest, which has a campervan waiting, leaving their victims supervised by a member of the cult. It is only a matter of time before the victim will be transferred to a desired hot spot, a destination for the ritual ceremony. Some require transportation overseas, which usually takes place through the smuggler's routes. The higher hierarchy also practises a format of an occult game and a tournament between the victims. To create cases of fabricated murders. This format is common for the elites to practise; the victim has to murder another victim in order to survive or to be murdered in a ceremony. It is not only tournaments that take place but also human medical experiments, mostly in agreement with the government. The victims lose their identities and history through the government database, ending up being ghosts. Then, they are being transferred to the military facilities where medical experiments are taking place.

New viruses and medicine are tested on the lab victims by military personnel and representatives from private medical establishments, such as Pfizer and AstraZeneca.It all started in 1946; the Roswell project was orientated on employing the Nazi scientists who were secretly working on viruses and used them on the captured German soldiers as their laboratory rats, whilst UFO was a distraction in order to keep the journalists and press investigating something else rather than a nearby facility.

The nature of the elites consists of a principle by which their partners can be liquidated. If one threatens another, it is a threat to all of them. As an example, a case of the Bavarian entrepreneur and an owner of one of the most known beer brands who was murdered in an occult ceremony with his wife and children. The contract was ordered by the one that was blackmailed with an exposition of security content. The victim was August Inselkammer Jr. He died apparently in a helicopter accident with his wife and children. However, did those events actually take place, or was it completely a different story from what was presented by the officials and media?

How did the Spanish government cause his death? Everything started with August and his threats to expose his partner in the higher hierarchy, one of the Pendars of the wealthiest German dynasties. August participated in a collective murder in which the Pendars of Germany and Spain took part. August was a person of morality and stood by the principles of humanity, so he decided to expose himself and others who were involved in the deal.

The previous king of Spain and his colleague, a pendar named Ernst August von Hannover, who represents the Bavarian elites, both decided to murder August and his family, hiding facts of his death by fabricating a story of a helicopter crash. An occult division working in the Spanish government had kidnapped him and his family only to

murder them in a ritual ceremony.

Everything else was a matter of fabrication, from the crash to the participation of the government and media conglomerates.

In priority of Zion, as much as in Masonry and Illuminati, exists a concept of Lucifer, an angel of light that must destroy all of Christianity and its belief as much as all other beliefs conducted by the churches. The belief in Lucifer and demons is threatening Christianity, and by the common plan, it must be destroyed by the events that are happening behind the scenes, such as paedophile lobbyists and the destruction of morals.

Meanwhile, in the Vatican, there are ritual sacrifices taking place with kidnapped toddlers. All of it benefits the Illuminati, Templar Knights, Masons and other organisations which believe in Lucifer.

Equilibrium as a part of the global conspiracy is only a tiny element in what is about to happen, which is a third world war against Russia and China. The plan consists of the western hysteria at first which is reflected in politicians calling for more security investment into NATO and the western ally nations, then a call for mobilisation despite no threat from the East. The Zionists that execute equilibrium against Palestine will also attack Iran in the future in agreement with Western organisations and elites. It is a developed plan of the Illuminati, which was planned two hundred years ago to start three world wars. As the Illuminati claims, they are spreading light and represent the Antichrist and demons, which are constantly in contact with them through meditation and taking drugs. They believe that their ideas come directly from invisible entities and are truthful, ideas which require repeating the historical cycle of Armageddon; their ancestors already had nuclear weapons in the past, but historians, who are part of the secret organisations, cover up the facts.

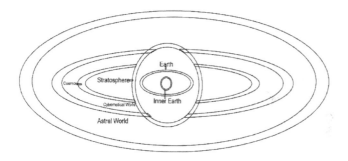

This is an example of our world; through the Astral projections, Illuminati claims to communicate with each other as much as with the demonic entities from inner earth and outer space.

The other cults, such as the cult of Shiva, which is controlled by the Illuminati, operate the modern CERN Facilities and have ritual sacrifices executed every month, with at least two victims being murdered. Their plan is by the middle of the first century to cause a mass sacrifice of its own cult members by setting an explosion to their CERN mechanism. Their other practises are finding a portal to the Cybernetical and Astral world on a physical level as they believe in mystical origins of the universe and in demonic substances that dictate them to research the Big Bang theory in order to open that portal and let the demons into our realm. How stupid and naive those cult members are is only for the viewer's judgment, but it costs a price of human life, serving entities that do not exist by taking psychedelic drugs and having their brains playing games with them as brain functions, linguistics, knowledge and experience dictates their minds to believe in what is not real but a result of their drug addictions.

Meanwhile, in Great Britain, there is a hidden game taking place to destroy the control of the Anglo Americans and Anglo-Scottish mason's power source, which is Scotland. The main plan is to split Scotland with the rest of Great Britain through a controlled SNP party which serves the Rockefellers. The Rockefellers were planning to split Scotland and Wales as well as unify Northern Ireland with Ireland by investing in the Irish separatists.

Those terror acts indirectly involved the Rockefellers, who cannot stand the Anglo-Americans and Anglo-Scottish Masons; the masonry itself is split, and there is no direct control of the Scottish or British order, which is controlled by the Bank of Englands lodge over the separate American Masonry. The masons are told to deny the fact that the Illuminati exists as their powers are limited in comparison to the majority of the Illuminati in the powerhouse of the United States with their allies of Skull and Bones. Brexit was a part of the plan to divide power in Great Britain; now, masons are desperate to keep it by having an alternative to the conservative party, which is the Reform Party UK. Masons and their Anglo-American allies used to control the conservative government, but then the power shifted towards their colleagues Illuminati, which masons secretly despise. The power shift is happening today, whilst the German National Party attempts to re-establish their links with old Nazi Allies such as Japan and Spain, with more deaths and securities taking place for these purposes. The Bank of Vatican remains neutral as an Italian sovereign entity, with a part of them integrated with the Illuminati to achieve their goals, but this is the separatist Illuminati fraction, which does not follow the main agenda of causing Armageddon. Meanwhile the elites of Zionists, Masons, Illuminati, Skull and Bones, Germans, Thule society and others prepared for the upcoming World War Three with the use of nuclear weapons as the civilians will choose their parties regardless of their views as they consider the population to be a stock of sheep.

Civilians are sheep that need to be controlled; their culture must develop in accordance with the plan, which involves the prevention of spiritual progress in favour of consumerism. Capitalism in its form, as much as the economy, must be sustained before it collapses with a spiritual awakening of the people to what is happening and who really controls the world. From retro styles to music, it's all part of the cultural degradation which promotes capital machines, and you, as slaves of the system, will obey and consume what will be presented. If a war starts, you won't protest but sit on your bottom, believing the propaganda machine and finding external enemies of the Elites. The only way out is to have decent people in the government and corporations, which lacks it completely as most of them are members of cults and secret societies. Decent people sell their souls to demons, zionists, elites and other established entities for money, for safety, and for control. They all perceive the world as a big chess board in which they have to develop strategies to overcome disagreements with their colleagues or to establish their liberal democratic values by starting a war and getting rid of the other governments. You can say that there is no point or purpose for wars, but it's human nature and greed, ideology and belief that is a virus in our society which cannot be eradicated as being a part of freedom of speech, choices and values. You cannot prove anything; you cannot accuse us of crimes against humanity as you have no evidence in comparison to us who execute crimes and murder innocent people. You will die by living in your own limbo and social environment, which is dictated by us. This is a primary rule of the Bilderberg Club, which serves as a negotiating platform between the secret societies.

Bildersberg group was formed by the Rockefellers and consists mainly of the Illuminati. The Zionists gathered in Tel Aviv for their international Jewish congress, but how did Zionism start, and who was the first group? You need to thank the Rothschilds for it; they and the Zionists are allies who established their relationships when the Warburgs were invested in their banking industry. The Rothschilds played an important part in the creation of Israel and Palestine by investing in both the Nazis and the Zionists at the same time prior the world war three; they are the cause of

events such as crystal night due to their investment into the Nazi Party, whilst their and Warburg's plan was to have a new settlement based in Palestine, with the Nazis prosecuting the Jews and leaving them no option but to escape Europe to find a safe place. Warburgs today have control of the US Federal Reserve as they continue to dominate the Zionist Jewish Congress and as much manipulate processes such as the war in the Gaza Strip. They originally came from a wealthy background from Venice,

Italy and migrated to Warburg, from which they have acquired a new name for themselves; they and the Rothschilds have a control package in the US Federal Reserve as well as the Rockefellers through JP Morgan, which use to be Anglo Scottish entity and then transformed into the entity of western Illuminati. They are all sinister as they invested millions in the Second World War, only to cause mass depopulation and sacrifices through the equilibrium concepts which was agreed upon by the Baruchs. From mass control over the population quantity to secret laboratories which specialised in infecting the hosts with cancer cells, this was done through Puerto Rico by the Rockefellers, which used the island as a part of their laboratory, practising new viruses, cancer and eugenics. They are all pendars and decide the route by which history will flow.

Great Britain used to be controlled by the Round Table Society, but after two thousand, it went into the administration of Skull and Bones with the Western Illuminati. Today, there are no alternatives but to choose between the Zionists-controlled Labour Party and the Western Illuminati, as those two entities run the nation. Masons lost their power and had only control of finances through the Bank of England and their HSBC Banking Society. Central London is the place from which the Round Table, masons and other associations manipulated the processes in International affairs, but today, they are powerless. Control over the population quantity is their priority, through the lobby of abortion supporters to a practical murder with the use of chemicals, such as Monsanto and Dupont Dow, an agreement between the Nazis of Bayer and Canadian Americans. To regulate, Monsanto introduced glyphosate, a dangerous chemical for agricultural use which causes cancer; the lobby of Nazi Bayer in the US Congress protects the company and the use of this chemical as most of them represent secret societies or are manipulated by them. No wonder you see those that spread abortion agenda to the mass audience, it's all part of the demographic management.

Their doctrine is to rule the world and manage us as the population grows and awakening is happening. More people are becoming aware of what is actually happening and decide to take action through voting for alternative political parties, but they have to be careful not to select monopoly-based ones as they are under the management of secret societies and their members.

Manufactured by Amazon.ca
Bolton, ON

39573945R00037